To Liz —
fair skies and full sails

First edition 2004

Library of Congress Cataloging-in-Publication Data
Kvasnosky, Laura McGee.
Frank and Izzy set sail / Laura McGee Kvasnosky. — 1st ed.
p.  cm.
Summary: Frank the bear and Izzy the rabbit sail
to Crescent Island and camp overnight.
ISBN 0-7636-2146-3
[Sailing — Fiction. 2. Camping — Fiction. 3. Bears — Fiction. 4. Rabbits — Fiction.] I. Title.
PZ7.K975Fr 2004
[E] — dc22       2003055454

2 4 6 8 10 9 7 5 3 1

Printed in Singapore

This book was typeset in Alghera.
The illustrations were done in gouache resist.

Candlewick Press
2067 Massachusetts Avenue
Cambridge, Massachusetts 02140

visit us at www.candlewick.com

# Frank & Izzy Set Sail

## Laura McGee Kvasnosky

CANDLEWICK PRESS
CAMBRIDGE, MASSACHUSETTS

Frank was practicing his ukulele
when the doorbell rang.
*Oh no*, he thought, *it's that rabbit again*.

He cracked open the door.

"Why, Frank," said Izzy. "I didn't know you play the ukulele. How about a song?"

Frank hid the ukulele behind his back.

"I'll sing along," said Izzy. "We can start a band! We'll be famous!"

Frank felt too shy to play his ukulele in front of anyone, especially Izzy. He changed the subject. "Would you like some lemonade?"

Frank and Izzy sat on the porch and sipped lemonade.

"I came by to see if you want to go sailing," said Izzy.

"Sounds interesting," said Frank. "I've read a lot about sailing." Then he remembered. Stories of shipwrecks and castaways.

"Well—" he began.

"You'll love it," Izzy said. "We'll sail to Crescent Island and camp overnight on the beach."

Frank squirmed. Sailing and sleeping out—yikes!

"Let's go get packed," said Izzy. She hopped off the porch.

Frank rose slowly. *At least she forgot about the ukulele,* he thought.

Frank laid out his stuff.

Toothbrush,

sleeping bag,

first-aid kit,

life jacket,

beach chairs,

rock collection,

food,

pots and pans,

flashlight,

extra batteries,

*Model Railroad* magazine,

bug spray.

The pile got bigger and bigger.

Pretty soon, Izzy was back with her tiny pack. She was humming — until she saw Frank's pile.

"We're only going for one night, Frank," she said.

"I like to be prepared," said Frank, but he put his rock collection back on the shelf.

"All this stuff will overload the boat," said Izzy.

"Maybe we could tow my gear in a dinghy," suggested Frank.

"Okay, okay," said Izzy.

Finally, Frank was packed.

"You load the wagon," said Izzy. "I'll zip up this red bag and be right out."

Frank and Izzy walked to the lake. Izzy talked the whole way.

"Do you know I hold the world record for singing the highest note?" she said.

She opened her mouth wide, but no sound came out.

"It's higher than you can hear," she said.

"Then how do you know it's the highest?" said Frank.

"I might have lied," said Izzy. "But let's not get bogged down in the facts."

At the dock, Izzy showed Frank how to rig the boat.

"Who taught you to sail?" he asked.

"My grandma," said Izzy. "She was a pirate and sailed the Seven Seas with a parrot on her shoulder."

"Really?" said Frank.

"Well, maybe not the parrot part," said Izzy.
She jumped into the boat and pushed off.

Frank held on for dear life.

Suddenly Izzy called, "Prepare to jibe."

Frank froze.

Then he remembered his reading. "Aye, aye," he answered, just like a real sailor.

"Jibe ho!" yelled Izzy. Frank ducked under the sail. The wind caught on the other side, and the boat skimmed across the lake.

Sailing to Crescent Island took most of the day because of the heavy dinghy.

"We can go exploring if we ever get there," said Izzy. "Maybe we'll find a sasquatch."

"A sasquatch," repeated Frank. "Isn't that a forest monster?"

Izzy nodded.

"You go ahead," said Frank. "I'll set up camp."

As soon as Frank pulled the boat up the beach, Izzy disappeared into the woods.

After a while, Frank put up the tent.
*When will Izzy be back?*
he wondered.

He began to make dinner.
It grew colder, darker. Scarier.
Still there was no sign of Izzy.

Frank sang a little tune to comfort himself.
*I wish I had my ukulele,* he thought.

CRACK! SNAP!

Something was crashing through the bushes.
It came closer! And closer!

Out limped Izzy.

"Am I glad to see you!" said Frank.

"I hurt my paw," wailed Izzy.
"A sasquatch bit it."

"Really?" said Frank.

"Just a baby sasquatch," said Izzy.

"I have just the thing," said Frank.

Frank bandaged Izzy's paw. Then
he ladled out hot tomato soup.

"Thanks," said Izzy.

Frank served chocolate pudding
for dessert.

"You thought of everything, Frank,"
said Izzy. She licked her bowl.

Frank and Izzy sat by the campfire.

"The only thing that could make this better is a song," said Izzy.

"Yes," said Frank. "I kind of wish I brought my ukulele."

Izzy grinned. "I guess you haven't looked in your red bag yet," she said. "Because you did!"

Frank hugged his ukulele. "Thanks, Izzy," he said.

He began to strum and sing softly. "Hoppy days are here again. . . ."

Izzy joined in. Loudly. Frank added harmonies and fancy strums.

Frank and Izzy sang to the stars.

In the morning, Izzy's paw was still sore. "I'm not sure I can handle the tiller," she said.

Frank gulped. "I'll give it a try."

The boat zigzagged up the lake as Frank figured out the rudder and the sail.

"See why I love sailing?" said Izzy.

Frank started to sing. "My bunny lies over the ocean. . . ."

Izzy chimed in.

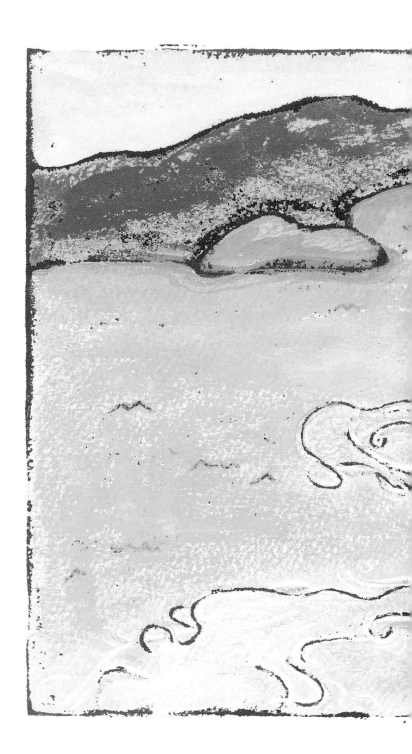

Eventually, Frank sailed alongside the dock.

Izzy helped with the landing.

"Good sailing!" she said. "And that's no lie!"

"Thanks," said Frank. "Could be my grandma
was a pirate, too."

That evening Frank and Izzy relaxed on the porch.

"Sometimes the best part of an adventure is coming home," said Frank.

"Maybe so," said Izzy.

After a song or two, Izzy turned to Frank. "We really could be stars," she said. "Let's try out for the Talent Show."

Frank strummed a few chords. "I don't know," he said. "We'd need lots of practice." He smiled at Izzy. "But we do sound pretty good together."

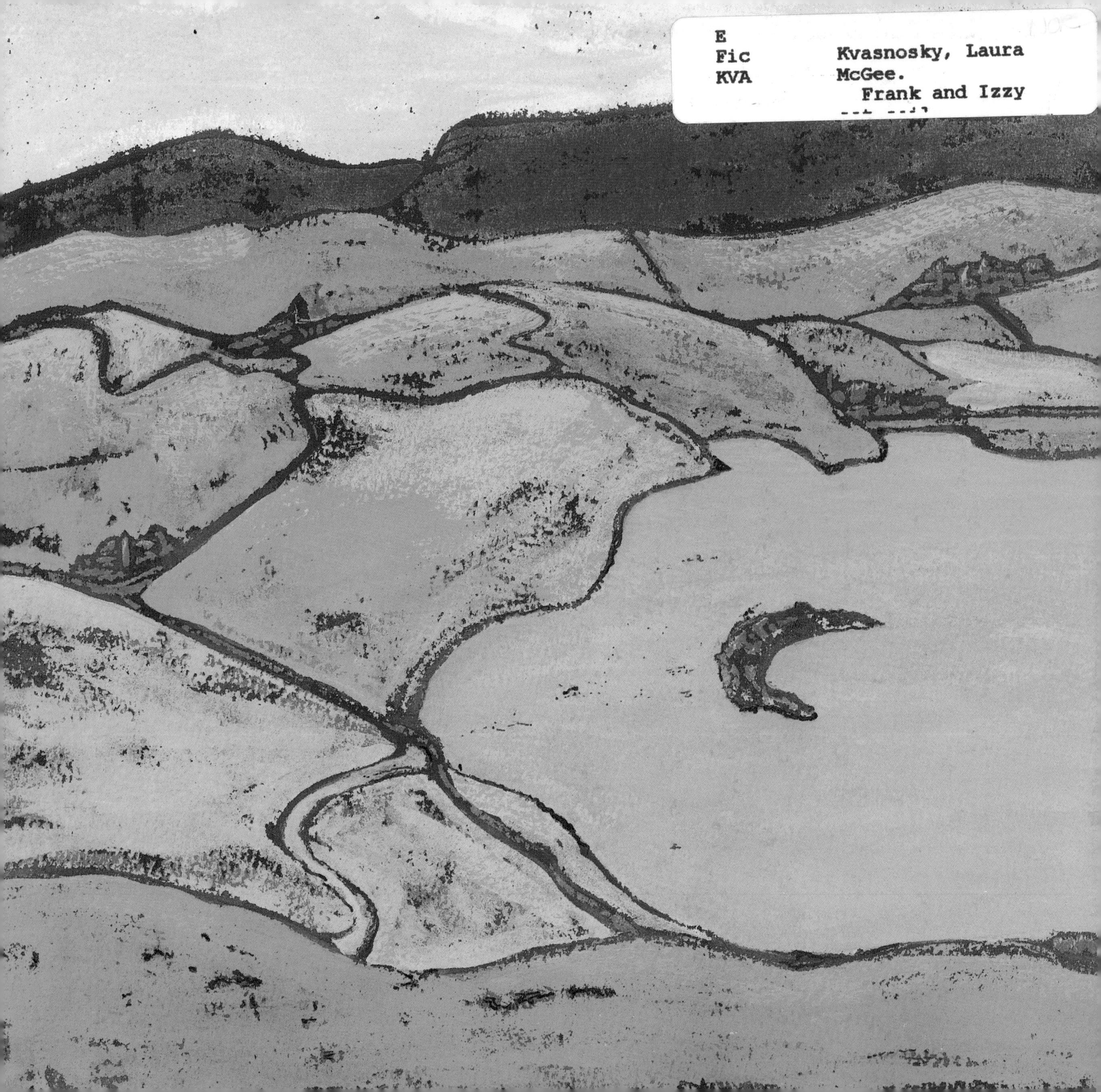